To Caitlin –
Wishing you health,
happiness, and
bluebonnets!

♡, Ellen
Leventhal

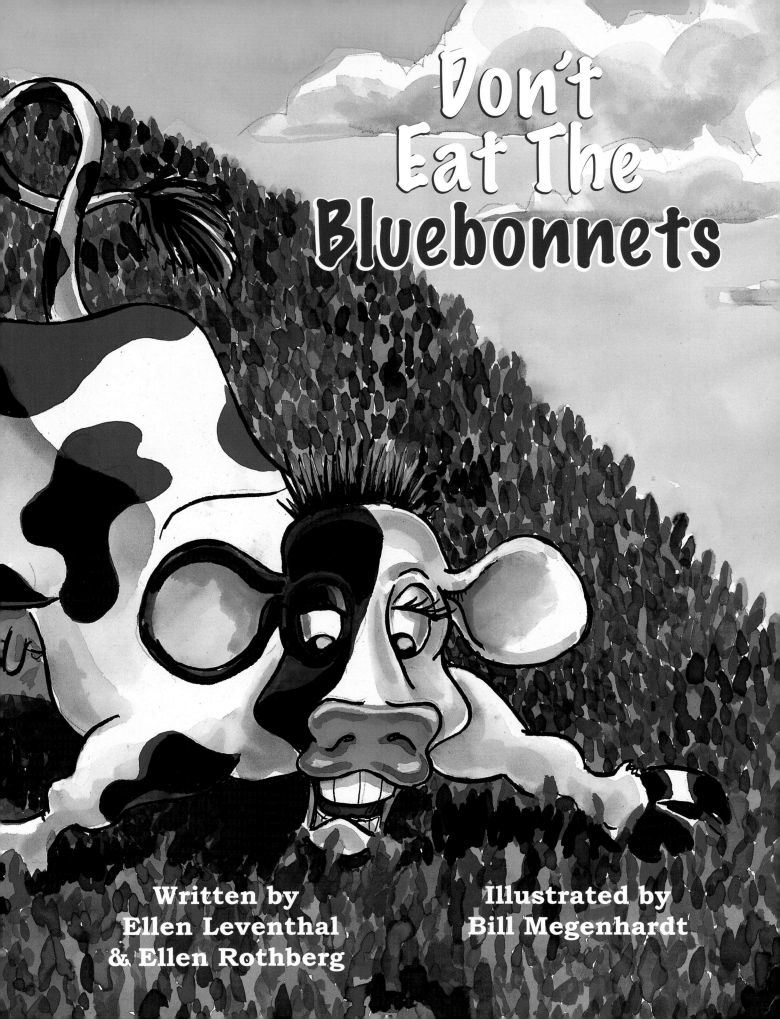

Don't Eat The Bluebonnets

Written by
Ellen Leventhal
& Ellen Rothberg

Illustrated by
Bill Megenhardt

For a cow, Sue Ellen had a mind of her own.
When the other cows mooed, Sue Ellen whistled.
When Max, the Longhorn, gave an order, all the
cows snapped to attention—except Sue Ellen.
She just swished her tail, batted her lashes, and
smelled the daisies.

DON'T EAT THE BLUEBONNETS

Every spring Max puts up a sign in Sue Ellen and Lisa Jean's favorite pasture.

"Humph," Sue Ellen said. "Max is not the boss of me. He can't tell me what to do." With that she hooked tails with Lisa Jean and they sashayed across the field.

"I can eat the bluebonnets if I want to," she snorted.

"The bluebonnets won't come back next spring if you eat them," Lisa Jean warned.

"But we eat the grass, and it comes back," Sue Ellen argued.

"That's true," replied Lisa Jean, "but bluebonnets are different. They won't come back."

Having a mind of her own, Sue Ellen wasn't totally convinced. The next day when Sue Ellen and Lisa Jean arrived at the south pasture, the bluebonnets were just starting to pop up. Sue Ellen's mouth watered.

"Don't forget. We're not supposed to eat the bluebonnets, " Lisa Jean reminded her.

"I'm not eating them. I'm just looking at them," Sue Ellen said, licking her lips.

As they stood beside the pond, Sue Ellen stuck her nose in the air and took a deep breath. "Don't the bluebonnets smell yummy?"

"Don't eat the bluebonnets," Lisa Jean reminded her.

Sue Ellen licked her lips again. "I'm not eating them. I'm just smelling them." She swished her tail. "Water comes back to the pond every year, doesn't it?" she muttered.

Later as Sue Ellen and Lisa Jean were grazing in the shade of the big oak tree, Sue Ellen noticed one small, perfect bluebonnet. It looked delicious. Her mouth watered.

"Don't eat the bluebonnets," Lisa Jean reminded her. Sue Ellen stuck her tongue out and licked the perfect flower. "I'm not eating it. I'm just licking it."

She looked up at the trees and swished her tail. "The leaves on the trees come back every year, don't they?" she said. "So do the birds," said Sue Ellen as they watched the mockingbirds teach their babies to fly.

"I guess they do," Lisa Jean said as she watched each baby leave the nest and return safely.

By the end of the week, the bluebonnets covered the pasture, and Sue Ellen couldn't stop thinking about them. She imagined how the petals would taste sliding down her throat. Sue Ellen thought about the water in the pond, she remembered the leaves coming back every spring, and she watched the birds fly by. And with that she charged into the south pasture and ate every single bluebonnet.

Sue Ellen was so full she had to lie
under the big oak tree and take a nap.
  When Sue Ellen opened her eyes,
Max was standing over her.
  "Humph," complained Max,
"Somebody ate all the bluebonnets!"
  "So what? They'll just grow back
next year."
  "Sometimes nature needs some
help," Max mumbled.
  "We'll just wait and see,"
yawned Sue Ellen.
So they waited.

The spring faded.

The summer came and went.

In the fall the leaves fell.

The winter chill blew in from the north.

Sue Ellen and Lisa Jean thought spring would never come. Then the days began to grow longer and the snow started to melt.

When the spring grass grew so tall that it tickled their bellies, they knew it was time to head to the south pasture where the bluebonnets grew.

When they reached the pasture that morning, they saw Max carrying his sign.

"Well, Sue Ellen, I guess we won't be needing this sign since the bluebonnets haven't grown back," Max bellowed.

All the cows glared at Sue Ellen.

Having a mind of her own, Sue Ellen decided
to take charge. "If the bluebonnets won't
come back," she thought, "I'll bring them back
myself." With that she swished her tail and
headed to the north pasture to gather some of
the bluebonnets growing there. "Bluebonnets
are bluebonnets," she said. "I'll just move the
bluebonnets from the north pasture to the
south pasture."

By midday the bluebonnets had wilted and
were so flat that even the bees couldn't find
the pollen in them.

Having a mind of her own, Sue Ellen decided to take charge. "Bluebonnets are bluebonnets. I'll just paint them on the hay," she thought as she grabbed her paints.

As Sue Ellen finished painting the last bale of hay, she glanced up and exclaimed in shock, "Well, that isn't going to work for long!"

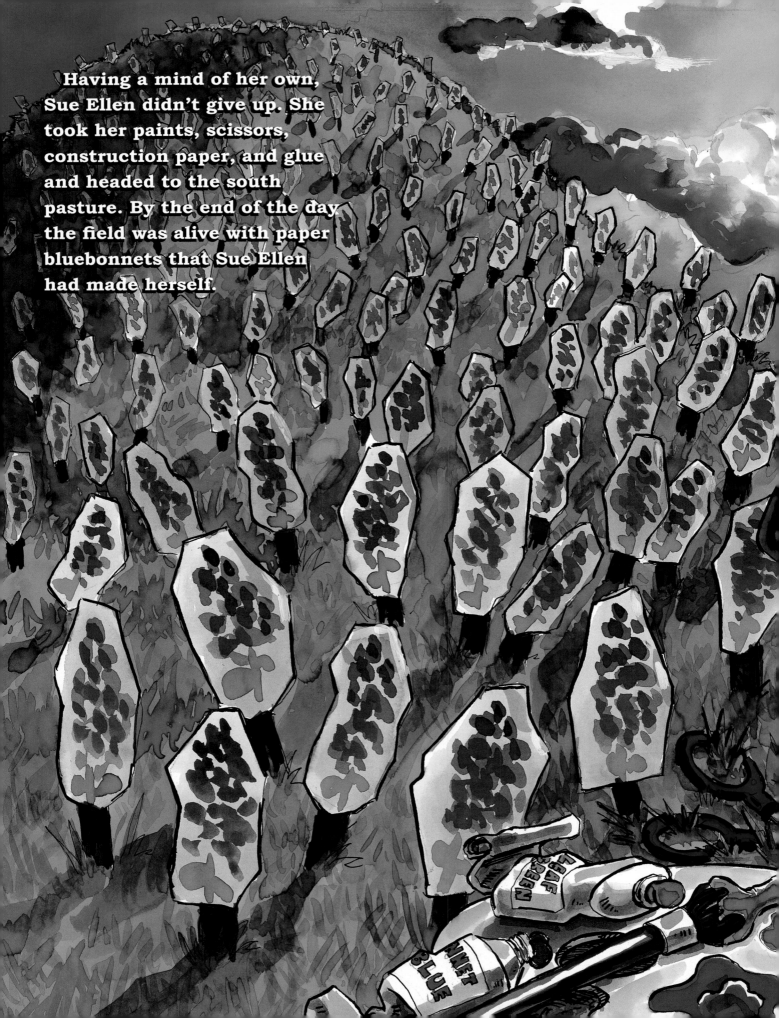

Having a mind of her own, Sue Ellen didn't give up. She took her paints, scissors, construction paper, and glue and headed to the south pasture. By the end of the day the field was alive with paper bluebonnets that Sue Ellen had made herself.

That night, a Texas size thunderstorm woke Sue Ellen up. Lightning lit up the sky, the thunder boomed, and the rain soaked the ground.

When Sue Ellen and Lisa Jean
got to the pasture the next
morning, the paper bluebonnets
had blown away.
"I guess only real bluebonnets
are the blue of the sky. And
only real bluebonnets have that
wonderful smell. And only real
bluebonnets are worth licking,"
she sighed.

So, having a mind of her own, Sue Ellen decided to take charge. That night she went to the south pasture and planted a packet of Max's seeds she had found in the barn.

When the next spring came,
Sue Ellen took out her paints
and freshened up Max's sign.
"Max," she said, batting her
lashes, "Will you please put
the sign up again?"
He laughed. "There's no
need. The bluebonnets won't
be back."

Having a mind of her own, Sue Ellen decided to take charge. She took the sign and planted it firmly in the ground where Max had put it before.

It wasn't long before their favorite pasture was beautiful again.

Having a mind of her own, Sue Ellen decided she could

. . . look at the bluebonnets

. . . smell the bluebonnets

. . . lick the bluebonnets. . .

but she could not eat the bluebonnets.

Bill Megenhardt has drawn pictures ever since he can remember. He is an illustrator living in Houston, Texas with his son Michael.

Ellen Rothberg wrote and illustrated her first children's book with a friend at the age of 7, and although she no longer draws the pictures, she still likes to write with her friend, Ellen Leventhal. She is a former elementary school teacher and currently works as an elementary school guidance counselor. She and her husband both love cows, bluebonnets, and their two grown children.

While growing up in New Jersey, **Ellen Leventhal** didn't dream of bluebonnet fields, but she did dream of writing books. Ellen has a master's degree in education and has been writing for and with her students for many years. She lives in Houston, Texas with her husband and is the proud mother of two grown sons, who love bluebonnets, Longhorns, and just about anything Texan.

Sue Ellen lives on a ranch in Texas with her little sister Lisa Jean, a herd of other cows, and a longhorn steer named Max. She now looks forward to the spring each year.

Authors' Notes

While cows can eat bluebonnets without harm, they can sometimes be toxic to other animals including humans.

Second printing 2009
13-Digit ISBN# 978-0-9820278-0-6
PCCN# 2008939509

Ellen Leventhal -- [1951-]
Ellen Rothberg -- [1956-]
Bill Megenhardt -- [1958-]
        Don't Eat The Bluebonnets / by Ellen Leventhal
                                and Ellen Rothberg
        Illustrator Bill Megenhardt -- 2nd ed.
        p.cm.
        SUMMARY: Sue Ellen eats all the bluebonnets and must solve the problem of getting them to come back the next spring.
        Audience: Ages 3-8.
        ISBN# 978-0-9820278-0-6 (hardback with jacket)
        1. Nature -- Juvenile Fiction.
        2. Problem Solving -- Juvenile Fiction.
        3. Consequences -- Juvenile Fiction. 1.Title.

The paper used in this publication meets the requirements of the American National Standard for Permanence of Paper for Printed Library Materials Z39.48-1984.
                        Printed in Canada

The ABC's Press
PO Box 19632
Houston, TX 77224-9632
713-937-9184 — fax: 713-896-9887
www.ABCsPress.com

Illustrations & Cover Design — Bill Megenhardt
Book Packager — Rita Mills of the Book Connection
www.bookconnectiononline.com
Editor — Kathi Appelt

Second Round Winner of
ABC's Children's Picture Book Competition
www.ABCbookCompetition.org